MW00479144

What people are saying about *Lucky Leo*...

'*Lucky Leo* *is a tenacious dog who survives adversity to pursue his hunting talent. The author, Pat Becker, has created a canine hero for this lively tale that will appeal to both young adults and dog lovers.* '

— Kent F. Frates, *award-winning Oklahoma author*

'*Becker skillfully weaves an argument for more responsible dog ownership with the intriguing world of sporting dogs. A meaningful and at the same time entertaining book for animal lovers of all ages.* '

— Darl DeVault, *Distinctly Oklahoma Magazine*

Lucky Leo
Copyright © 2017 by Pat Becker
Story by Pat Becker
Cover art and illustrations by Sherry Brown-Judy

The author of this book will always try to accommodate a
book reading, speaking to a group, or appearing for a book
signing or an interview. For more information or to book
an event, contact Pat Becker at:
info@patbeckerbooks.com
or by phone at: (405) 627-9272

For more information about the writing of this book, the
background of the author or to order
autographed copies online:
www.patbeckerbooks.com

Publishing & printing
by Total Publishing and Media (Tulsa, Oklahoma)

This edition printed in 2017.

10 9 8 7 6 5 4 3 2 1

ISBN (HC): 978-1-63302-064-1
ISBN (eBook): 978-1-63302-065-8

TOTAL
PUBLISHING
& MEDIA

Dedication...

To the responsible, caring owners of game dogs: Would that all sporting dogs be so *lucky*.

Contents

Chapter 1: Abandoned   1

Chapter 2: A Hungry Pilgrim   9

Chapter 3: Fading Hope   18

Chapter 4: Change of Fortune   24

Chapter 5: Pride and Courage   32

CHAPTER

1

Abandoned

A FINAL BURST OF COLORS DANCED across the sky, splashing the atmosphere with brilliant shades of coral, pink, and blue green— a spectacular gift from the sun as it began its descent to the horizon.

It was on this kind of evening that a day of successful quail hunting left two middle-aged men contented and ready for a good dinner at Bob's Steakhouse—their favorite for many years. The two hunters checked their shotguns, put them in their cases, and unloaded the quail from their vests.

"Great day!" one of the men said.

"Yep!" said the other. "It don't get much better than this."

The two friends started loading the bird dogs into their kennels inside the custom-built trailer. "I think we're missing one, Frank," the tall, lanky man said as he counted heads and started looking around.

"I'll bet I know who," Frank replied. "That shorthair is the orneriest dog I've ever seen."

Phil shook his head. "He may be, but he's a heck of a big ranging dog—and he sure pointed his share of coveys today."

"Yeah, but he's just so darned undisciplined!" said Frank, clearly agitated. "About the time I think he's hitting his stride, he does

something stupid—like chomping a bird right after he's fetched five of 'em straight back to me and dropped 'em in my hand. Or staying with us for miles, then just running the other way as fast as he can with me blowing the bean outta my whistle. That ornery sucker can act fairly distant one day, and the next day he's wanting to be a lapdog."

Frank paused briefly and looked into the distance before continuing. "He gets along pretty well with the other pointers—till one of 'em looks at him the wrong way. Then he wants to fight! I'll have to say he's an athletic son of a gun. I swear he can jump a six-foot, chain-link fence that other dogs would find hard to climb."

The hunter shook his head and turned back to his friend. "He's got the stride of a horse and the stamina of a cougar. He's got as good a nose as any bird dog I've ever seen, except if he decides one day that he isn't sure that's where he wants to be. Then he's quit on ya! I'm telling ya, Phil, I'm not sure that he's worth the trouble."

"Well, we're pretty much through for the day," Phil said. "We gonna wait for him, or

what?" The older man was feeling tired and sore from the all-day hike they had taken. His feet were ready for a rest, and he could almost taste the steak at Bob's—and the cold beer. It was "Miller Time," and he was geared up for some major relaxing.

"You know what?" Phil said answering his own question. "I ain't waiting! No, sir—I ain't! I've put up with his go-to-heck attitude for the last time. We're outta here!" The truck and trailer lunged forward, and pulled through the gate of the pasture and onto the highway.

Ten minutes later a large German Short-haired Pointer ran from an adjacent pasture and down the sandy road to the spot where the Suburban had been parked. He was covered in burrs and breathing hard, all the while clinging to the quail held in his mouth.

He dropped the bird, and looked around bewildered and confused. It was almost dark now, and the sound of howling coyotes startled him. He couldn't understand what had happened. He sniffed the ground for clues. He ran to the road, then back to the place where his owner and the other dogs had been. He lifted his nose but could find no familiar scent on the night air. He combed the immediate area again and again.

The quail, which had eluded his search when it fell earlier in the day, had taken all his

persistence to find. Now it lay on the ground, forgotten.

His heart sank. This was his fourth season— not a lengthy career. He had no idea how to handle this kind of situation. He walked to the side of the sandy road and lay down to wait for his owner's return.

Thin rays of light from the morning sun broke through the trees surrounding the area where the big dog lay sleeping. A pair of meadowlarks flushed from a nearby plumb thicket, and the pointer jumped to his feet. Disoriented, he stood and watched as the birds landed a few yards away. The night had been cold. His sleep had been restless, and his body was stiff and sore.

His empty stomach rumbled as he recalled yesterday evening's events. The fact that he had been abandoned had not occurred to him. He

stretched and sat down on the now so-familiar spot and again waited for his owner. Surely the man would be pleased to see the retrieved bird and would reward him with an ample amount of food.

By noon his hunger was intense. By sunset he was beginning to feel weak. The quail became his first meal in many hours.

CHAPTER

2

A Hungry Pilgrim

THE NEXT MORNING, the young pointer decided to try to find his way home. He still could not understand the consequences of his predicament, which made him feel uncertain and fearful.

He walked for days, fortunate to run down an occasional rat or squirrel and to happen upon a pond of water. He avoided the highways and vehicle-crowded streets—a lesson he had learned when he barely escaped death from speeding cars on more than one occasion.

Three weeks passed, and he grew bone thin. His coat was grimy and his gait slow, yet his instincts pushed him on.

As he passed through a small town one night,

he spotted a bowl of dry dog food on a porch at the back of a church. He guzzled the kibble and lay down, falling asleep immediately.

Early the next morning he awoke with a start when the door opened suddenly. A lady with a broom in her hand began briskly sweeping the previous day's dust from the kitchen, off the porch, and down the steps. She failed to notice the sleeping pointer.

The poor dog was so frightened that he fell off the porch, landing in a heap on the bottom step. The startled woman jumped back into the kitchen. The dog sat dazed, too weak to run. The woman cautiously peered around the half-opened door and stared at the sad, bedraggled animal.

Her heart ached for the pitiful creature, and she knew she had to try to help him. "Oh, you poor thing!" she said. "You just wait here one minute, OK?"

She turned to go back into the kitchen. "Now don't go away. I'll be right back."

As confused and wary as the big dog was, he saw kindness in the woman's eyes, and her gentle manner was comforting to him. The door opened again, and the aroma of warm food filled his nostrils. A bowl was sat in front of him, and he eagerly gobbled its contents.

A man appeared beside the woman and looked down at the stray dog. "What's going on, Sara?"

"A poor hungry pilgrim, Father," she responded. "Will you give him a special blessing?" The woman smiled up at the tall priest.

"Sara, you could convert the devil," the man said with a laugh. "I say a prayer of thanks every day that you are on our side. Only one meal, then he's on his way. This parish can't afford to feed every lost animal who finds his way to our

back door."

The woman lowered her head shyly. "I'm afraid the word is out, sir, this is the fifth sad creature I've fed this month. I've prayed to Saint Francis so many times."

"That explains it then," the priest said. "He's made you his emissary." The kind priest put his hand on the chubby woman's shoulder. "He's a sad case, that's true. However, my dear Mrs. O'Conner, the rule still stands—one meal!" The priest turned to go.

Whether due to the dog's poor condition or the rapid consumption of the warm meal, his stomach began to churn. He gagged, heaved, and threw up his undigested breakfast, the putrid substance spilling onto the porch.

"Oh, my!" The priest put his hand to his mouth and ran back inside the door.

"Why you poor unhappy creature," Sara said softly. "You're ill."

The dog staggered away from the porch and lay down on his side.

"DOCTOR METZ, PLEASE," Sara said after dialing a local veterinarian. "It's Sara O'Conner from the church."

Amy, the pretty brunette receptionist, handed the phone to the veterinarian as he passed her desk. "I really don't know, Sara," the man said as he spoke into the receiver. "I'll have to see him. Bring him in about nine o'clock... Right...We'll see you then. Give my best to Father Kelly. Good-bye."

The veterinarian returned the phone to the young receptionist. "She's bringing in another stray," he said. "I'll check him out, but I'm not keeping and feeding another one."

"But, Dr. Metz..." the girl pleaded.

"Not one more!" scolded the disgruntled vet.

The dog was brought in, and true to his word Dr. Metz examined him thoroughly. "Well, he's malnourished and wormy," he advised Sara, "but he'll live. From all appearances, he's a well-bred German Shorthaired Pointer. Probably got lost...or abandoned while hunting."

"You mean left to die alone in an unfamiliar place?" Sara had tears in her eyes, "Who would do such a thing—and why?"

"Truth is, it happens all the time," the veterinarian said. "Most bird hunters take proper care of their dogs, but a dog who's gun shy, or chronically ill, or too old to hunt, isn't much use to some of the hard-hearted guys who couldn't care less. It's just one of those facts of life, Sara. Anyway, you take him back to the church and feed him well. You'll have a healthy, very grateful pet."

"You know the Father won't let me keep him," the little old lady said as she flashed her winning smile. "Can I leave him here until I find him a proper home?"

"Oh, no—absolutely not!" the young vet said. "I'm going broke from all the free room and board I give to the lost animals who manage to get dumped at the church."

"I know," Sara said dropping her head. "I understand what a burden it must be for you, but God has sent His creatures to us for help. How can we refuse Him?"

"To you, Sara!" the vet corrected. "God has

sent them to you. Not to me—because God knows that I am a mere mortal who doesn't have the time or the patience or the room for such insanity."

"Please, Dr. Metz," the woman begged. "This will be the last one. Look at the poor thing. You can see that he was once a proud hunting dog. And now he is broken and so sad. It isn't fair." Tears unashamedly rolled down her cheeks.

"There's a lot that's unfair in this world!" the vet exploded. "It isn't fair that I'm the only veterinarian in town whom you harass this way." The exasperated look on his face told Sara that he had indeed come to the end of his rope.

"Very well, I understand," she said. "God will bless you for your past kindness to all of the other helpless animals for whom you have cared. Good day, Dr. Metz."

Sara snapped an old lead to the dog's weathered hunting collar and helped him off the examination table. As the old lady and the dog reached the door, Dr. Metz hollered, "Two days! That's it! Two days then he goes to the shelter."

"Oh, praise the Lord!" Sara said excitedly. "God will surely bless you Charles Metz."

"I'm grateful for His blessing, Sara, but I'd be more grateful if He would find this dog a home."

Sara tried all of the usual sources that day, but to no avail. All of the rescue clubs were overcrowded, and the individuals whom she had prevailed upon in the past hadn't returned her calls. Father Kelly told her it was understandable, and warned her against being so "pushy."

At the end of the second day, Dr. Metz called to say that he was sending the dog to the shelter. Sara prayed all night long to Saint Francis to intervene in this matter.

CHAPTER

3

Fading Hope

THE BIG POINTER STRETCHED in the large crate and ate the ration of food given him by one of the clinic's attendants. Amy brought him a small chew bone, as she had before, and rubbed his coat with a rubber mitt. "You like that, don't you, boy," she said. "We've got to get you shiny so somebody will see how handsome you are and want to adopt you."

"I'm glad you're here so early, Amy," Dr. Metz said handing her the signed vaccination papers. "I need you to take that dog to the shelter today. I called them and made all of the necessary arrangements."

The young woman stared at him. "But...I thought..."

"You heard me tell Sara that I would give him two days. Well it's been two days."

"I know, but I didn't think that you meant it," Amy said rubbing the grooming glove between her hands."

Dr. Metz glared at her. "Take him and go—now!"

The young girl loaded the pointer into the back seat of her car and reached for her phone to call her best friend, La Donna. "You have to come with me, I can't do this by myself. I feel so terrible." Amy turned off her cell phone and let it fall to her lap as she leaned her head on the steering wheel of her car.

La Donna arrived a short time later and comforted her. "Maybe you could just refuse to do it," she offered. "You know, go on strike or something."

"Not likely!" Amy sobbed. "I need my job." The pointer leaned over the front seat and licked her cheek.

"He is a pretty dog," La Donna said leaning back to pet him, "and he seems so friendly. Oh, by the way, I called Jarrod. I thought that he might have some ideas."

A man's voice from outside the car startled them as he leaned against the car door. "I might know of somebody," the young man said. "Is this the dog?"

He reached through the window and stroked

the dog's ears. The pointer cocked his head and came closer. He looked deep into the man's eyes, whined, and gently licked his outstretched hand.

"Jarrod!" Amy said dabbing at her eyes. "I'm so glad you're here."

"Who's the person you thought of?" La Donna asked Jarrod as she opened the car door for him.

Jarrod climbed into the back seat with the dog. "Man! You know what—this is a cool dog!" The young man flashed a wide smile, revealing deep dimples on his cheeks that added to his good looks. His gray eyes sparkled with animation. His physical features hinted at his Native American heritage.

"Then why don't you take him?" Amy asked.

Jarrod looked thoughtfully at the stray animal and exchanged glances with La Donna. "Nah, we can't have pets in the duplex."

"Maybe your mom would want him," Amy persisted.

Jarrod raised an eyebrow and laughed. "Yeah, right! I don't think he and Mom's dog would get along. But this man I work for might be interested."

"Does he like hunting dogs?" Amy asked. "Dr. Metz thinks that this dog's a pretty well-bred bird dog. So he'll probably need a big place to run. I really like this dog, Jarrod. I want to find him a good home."

Amy was starting to tear up again.

"Well, if Jim Williams won't take him," Jarrod said, "I'll bet that he'll have some friends who might. This could take some time." The big dog relaxed against Jarrod's shoulder.

"No, we don't have time," Amy moaned. "Dr. Metz told me to take him to the shelter

right now. If we can't find somebody to take him, I'll have to drop him off and they'll put him to sleep. When I called the shelter they said that hardly anybody ever adopts hunting dogs. He said that I should try to find someone to take him because his chances are slim to none. That's exactly the way he put it—'slim to none.'" Amy put her face in her hands.

"OK," Jarrod said, "Mike told me last night that he and Jim were going to Farmer's Grain to get some plants this morning. Let's go see if we can catch 'em. It's over on Third Street, I think. Drive over that way, and I'll show you."

CHAPTER

4

Change of Fortune

JARROD DIRECTED AMY to the nursery and grain store. As they pulled into the parking area at the front of the building, he spotted his best friend, Mike.

Mike was attending college and planning a career in landscape design. He spent most of his summer vacations at Jim's farm designing and planting gardens surrounding the house. He built small ponds and rock garden spots, laid concrete pavers, and placed cement benches, fountains and statuary around the yard. There were various ornamental trees, exotic bushes, and vivid-colored flowers. Jim's wife loved the additions.

"Hey!" Jarrod called as he approached

Mike, who was lifting a flat of flowers into the back of the farm pickup.

The tall, muscular man grinned as he turned to see Jarrod. "What's going on?"

"Nothing—except La Donna and Amy have this hunting dog that they're trying to find a home for." Jarrod looked down at his feet, then at the car where the pointer sat wagging his tail. "I thought Jim might take him."

Mike looked at Jarrod, then at the unfortunate pointer. "Oh, no—unh-uh. I'm not getting involved in this deal. Jim's got nine dogs. There's no way."

Jarrod smiled. "I know, but there's something about this dog. He looks pretty awful, but he's tough and proud—sorta like a soldier, or warrior, or somebody like that. He's kinda like...a sad lion."

"He's a dog, Jarrod, an animal who costs lots of money to take care of." Mike shook his head. "I don't think Jim's gonna go for it."

Jim finished chatting with the nurseryman Lesley in the feed store. He paid his bill and walked toward the truck. The two young men leaned against the tailgate looking sheepish.

"Hi, Jarrod, how are you?" Jim set the fern he was carrying on the tailgate of the pickup. Neither of the younger men spoke, both just grinning and nodding recognition.

"What?" Jim laughed.

Jarrod spat out the words tactlessly. "Jim, they're gonna put this dog to sleep, if you don't take him."

Mike rolled his eyes and said under his

breath, "Oh, man! Good going Jarrod!"

"A dog? What dog?" Jim asked.

"That dog," Mike said as he motioned and moved toward the car. Jarrod led the way. The pointer stuck his head out the window, giving Jim's hand a slurppy lick.

"Where did you find him?" Jim asked as he appraised the dog. "He's a German Shorthaired...a bird dog."

"Yeah!" Jarrod said happily. "I knew you'd

know that." He introduced his two friends, and Amy related the pointer's sad story.

"Well," Jim said, "I don't know. Chances are he's gun shy. If so, he won't hunt. And if he won't hunt..."

"He will," Jarrod said with a smile. "I know he will."

"Jarrod, you don't know that." Mike scowled and looked at Jim.

Amy got out of the car and stood by the open

door. "Mr. Williams," she said. "I'm on my way to take him to the shelter. I can't keep him. Jarrod and La Donna can't keep him. You're his only hope."

Jim looked at Jarrod. He admired the young man's love for animals, and he seemed to have a special communication with them.

"What do ya think, Mike?" Jim said leaning against the pickup. He studied the bird dog, whose head was out the window, his long tongue hanging from the side of his mouth.

Mike smiled and threw up his hands. He started walking back to the pickup as if to say, "I'm not taking any responsibility for this."

Jarrod continued his pleas. "Jim, this dog's special. I feel like I understand him. He's got pride—like a lion. He just needs somebody to help him with his confidence, someone to give him back his courage. Let him show you what a heck of a hunter he is."

"Well," Jim said, "Maybe you two are kindred spirits, Jarrod. OK...on your intuition I'll give him a chance. Put him in the truck."

"What're you gonna call him?" Jarrod asked loading the pointer into the pickup. "How about

Lion," he suggested.

Jim laughed. "I'll tell you what, I'll call him Leo...Lucky Leo."

"Yeah, that's perfect!" Jarrod said. "His luck is totally changing."

Leo demonstrated a great deal of zest for quail hunting and seemed to enjoy the attention lavished upon him. He regained his health and became fit enough to hunt with the other dogs in the group.

Jim admired the big dog's zeal and was pa-

tient with his training. After a few months Leo
began to express an attitude of attachment to his
new owner and the group of dogs with whom
he lived and hunted. His skills were honed, and
he improved with each season.

CHAPTER

5

Pride and Courage

A YEAR OR SO LATER ON A bright winter's day, Jim and Mike were hunting at a ranch known for its large quail population. The terrain was rugged with steep hills and deep valleys and the pastures were thick with shinnery—a scrub oak under which quail will hide.

Jim brought seven of his best dogs that day. Leo was included, an honor he earned from his consistent successes within the group. Suzy, an English Pointer-German Shorthaired crossbreed, took the lead and ranged far ahead. The dogs covered a lot of flat pasture areas and found several coveys. They worked well together, and Jim was proud of them all.

At noon, a small lunch and a little rest reenergized the group, and they continued their hunt, which took them into some of the more elevated areas. The uneven terrain made it more difficult to spot all of the dogs, but the two men finally caught up with them.

The dogs were "honoring" Suzy's point. She was again holding a covey—this time on the ridge of a cliff overlooking a steep drop to the valley below. Another ridge stood about two hundred feet across the way. Each dog held his position, forming a jagged line toward Suzy. As if frozen in time, every pointer 'locked–up,' waiting for that thrilling moment when the quail would burst into the air with a shattering sound.

"Wow!" Mike whispered. "I wish I'd brought my camera. Sights like this are worth saving. I don't think I've ever seen pointers honoring a point going up a steep hill this way."

The young man continued to stare at the vision. The descending sun's rays were now behind the group of dogs, who appeared almost shadowy. The sparse number of blackjack trees high on the side of the hill shined eerily.

"Can you get a shot, Mike?" Jim asked,

somewhat concerned about their ability to see clearly.

"Oh, yeah!" Mike whispered. "Just give me the chance."

As the two men moved up the hill, the other dogs backing Suzy were trembling in anticipation.

"I think all of us are anxious for that chance,"

Jim answered, "but we could have a little problem here, Mike. If we get a couple good shots from this angle, the quail may go over the cliff, and then the dogs can't retrieve them. We may lose our dinner. That gorge is pretty wide, and if some of the live birds fly across, it'll be impossible to find them."

Jim carefully scrutinized the terrain. "We'll have to go around this group of hills," he said, "and it'll take too long. It'll be getting dark soon. What do ya think?"

"Your dogs, your decision," Mike said.

"Well," Jim laughed, "we'll leave it to fate. We've all walked a long way for this covey. I say let's roll the dice." He stepped toward the covey and flushed them.

Twenty-five or so tiny quail erupted. Each man hit two. A couple did fly from the cliff and disappear from view.

"OK!" Mike said and laughed. "So much for my trying to get those headed away from the edge."

"It's fine," Jim replied. "We got pretty lucky with the ones we got. Nothing to sneeze at."

The men pocketed the quail in their vests as

the dogs retrieved them. As they were about to walk back to the truck and load the dogs into the trailer, Mike stopped to look across the gorge. "Wow! That sunset is something else. My gosh! I can't believe it!"

"Yeah!" Jim said joining him. "It's truly awesome, right?"

Jim continued staring at the thrilling scene. "Hey, wait a minute," he said. "The sunset's great, Mike, but what I'm also seeing is one of our dogs on the other side of that chasm."

"Oh, no!" Mike exclaimed. "Who is it?" He could see that Jim was seriously concerned.

"I think it's Leo," Jim said. "Let's count heads."

They called each dog, and all except Leo were there.

"OK, so it's Leo," Jim said. "I'll get the binoculars."

Leaning as far over the cliff as was safe, Jim focused on his wayward pointer. "He has a bird," he said. "I guess he picked it up from the other hill across the valley. He's coming down a path to the bottom. I think that we can drive around and intercept him. It'll take him a while to start up this hill. Let's get to the truck and trailer. The sun's about to set. We don't have much time."

Leo had seen the two birds fly over the cliff as they were flushed. In his enthusiasm, the impulsive pointer had jumped over the edge following the quail. Luckily he landed on a ledge, which slanted down to a path that wound its way to the bottom of the canyon.

One of the wounded quail had managed to glide from the cliff to the adjacent hill. Leo ran across the valley floor and leaped upon a large rock on which the quail lay. He picked it up and jumped from the boulder, pausing to look ahead for the path he needed to return.

Suddenly a familiar sound stirred his senses. The coyotes had begun their evening hunt, their voices echoing across the area. In the distance clouds had formed, and thunder indicated an approaching storm. The eerie, plaintive calls of the coyotes triggered memories of that sad day when he was left to survive on his own. The horrific experience still haunted him.

He started to panic as he ran across the canyon to the hill on which he had left his friends.

He still carried his bird, his gift to Jim. The sun had taken its final burst of color as it slid to the horizon. The shadows made the incline more difficult to see.

Groping the slick rocks, he clawed his way up the steep hill, slipping occasionally and falling into thorny bushes along the way. When he finally reached the ledge from which he had originally jumped, he suddenly realized that

the overhang protruded so far from the top that it was impossible to climb.

It was very dark now, and the thunder seemed louder, the storm closer. The poor dog lay down, put his head between his paws, and closed his eyes. He knew that he had made a terrible mistake. He trembled with anxiety.

Jim and Mike drove through the canyon and parked at the bottom of the tall hill on the east side. They started walking, checking up and down the area with flashlights and binoculars in hand.

Looking high up the hill, Jim spotted Leo. "I

see him, Mike! Let's get him down here. Leo!
Leo! Come here, boy!"

The big dog jumped to his feet as he heard
Jim's voice and excitedly ran down the hill toward him.

"Here he comes!" Jim shouted. "Dang it if
he doesn't have a bird. Look at that! Good boy,
Leo."

Jim held out his arms, and Leo ran to him. "Kind of a scrawny bird you've been hanging on to, you silly dog," Jim said. "But you get an "A" for the retrieve. Yep, you're a winner, Leo, a super addition to our group. I love your enthusiasm. We have some great seasons of quail hunting ahead of us."

Leo rubbed his head against Jim's chest and

sighed. His fear was gone, his confidence restored. He would never again have to worry or wonder about his future. ❑

Lucky Leo: a dog who recovered his pride and courage

The fully recovered Leo became a favorite hunting dog to his owners, Pat and Jim. The lucky sporting dog lived out his life both loved and honored on an estate north of Edmond, Oklahoma.

Pat Becker of Edmond, Oklahoma, has a career that has spanned movies, television and radio. She produced and narrated the award-winning series "The World of Dogs" for the Public Broadcasting Service. She is the author of the recently released children's series *Bandit and Company*, and author of the young-adult book *Bodacious Bo: The Pound Prince*, which followed her first book, *The Search for Paradise*. She also has produced a popular sing-along, multi-media book, *I Love Being Me*, which is celebrated in public school in several states.

Dog ownership and its responsibility have been an ongoing project and passion for the active owner of a variety of dogs. Currently, Pat produces and hosts the lively television show "Dog Talk" on KAUT Channel 43 in Oklahoma City.

All of Pat's books are available for purchase online at:
www.PatBeckerBooks.com

To the readers...

I sincerely hope that you enjoyed this story of Lucky Leo's journey to find a forever home with folks who could understand and value his hunting skills.

Sporting breed dogs make great companions while in the field, or cuddling at home!

There are so many wonderful breeds of pointers and retrievers from which to choose. Please remember to check rescues and shelters for those who have been lost or abandoned...like LEO!

Pat Becker

Other works by Pat Becker...

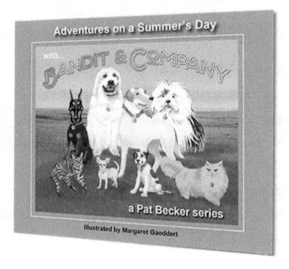

'*With her usual imaginative flair, Pat Becker brings to life this new series about a band of pet dogs and cats and their adventures in a loving home in an ideal setting. Readers of all ages will smile within when they recognize the human qualities the author has imbued in all these animals. ...*

The stunning color illustrations by artist Margaret Gaeddert add greatly to the character development and narrative. ...'

— Darl DeVault, Executive Editor
Distinctly Oklahoma Magazine

Purchase at www.PatBeckerBooks.com

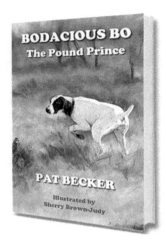

Crossbred between English and German Shorthaired pointers, precocious puppy Bodacious Bo appears destined for fame in the world of field-trial champions. But misfortune strikes, pushing young Bo into a harsh world far different from the life he had been groomed for. He finds himself in the unforgiving world of nature where his instinctive skills as a sporting dog will be used for survival. Fate returns him to the complicated world of people, where he searches for a "forever home" and to fulfill his destiny as a champion in the world of sporting dogs.

'A captivating read for all dog lovers...a bittersweet tale of adventure, loss and love. The illustrations are charming!'

— Marilyn King, Publisher
TulsaPets Magazine & OKC Pets Magazine

Purchase at www.PatBeckerBooks.com

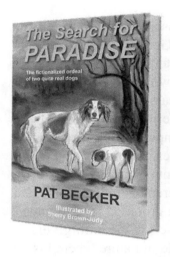

Separated from her puppies by a cruel farmhand, the grieving Brittany pointer Dixie comes to the aid of a traumatized English pointer puppy. The sad little pup's deceased mother had been Dixie's best friend. Dixie vows to her lost friend that she will take good care of her orphaned puppy. Leaving behind the farm that had brought them so much suffering, the two dogs embark on a journey that Dixie says will lead "to a better place...a wonderful place... Paradise."

Can Dixie fulfill her pledge to take good care of the vulnerable puppy? Will they ever find the wonderful home that Dixie calls Paradise?

'It's part thriller, part sad, part uplifting. It caught my attention from the get-go and kept it...'

— Marilyn King, Publisher
TulsaPets Magazine & OKC Pets Magazine

Purchase at www.PatBeckerBooks.com

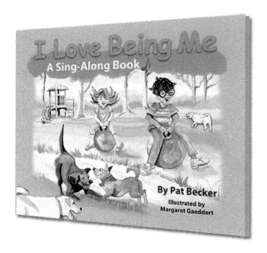

Sing Along to...

I Love Being Me
(multi-media entertainment)

Children of all ages will enjoy singing these positive lyrics and viewing these delightful illustrations. This multi-media entertainment package can be enjoyed by groups large or small, or even by a child alone.

DVD & Book
As you view the DVD, sing along
to the illustrated lyrics!

Purchase at www.PatBeckerBooks.com

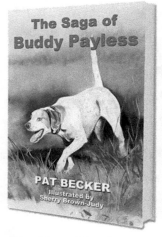

A cocky, young English Pointer destined for greatness in the world of quail hunting has little tolerance or interest in others—whether human or his own dog companions. But on his way to stardom in the world of game dogs, the talented bird dog suffers a cruel setback at the hands of heartless dog thieves. The little pointer learns to care about more than himself as he tries to make sense of a new world where he is no longer in control of his fate.

Can he find his way back to the familiar world of quail hunting, caring owners, and trusty companions? Or will he wander in life, never fulfilling his destiny as a champion sports dog?

'Pat Becker scores again with her unique insight into the feelings and emotions of dogs fighting to survive in a world controlled by people...'

— Darl DeVault, Executive Editor
Distinctly Oklahoma Magazine

Purchase at www.PatBeckerBooks.com